Hide and Peep

FAIRY SCHOOL

Hide and Peep

by Gail Herman

illustrated by Fran Gianfriddo

A Skylark Book

New York • Toronto • London • Sydney • Auckland

RL 2.5, AGES 006–009

HIDE AND PEEP

A Bantam Skylark Book / June 2000

ISBN: 0-553-48710-8

Visit us on the Web! www.randomhouse.com/kids
Educators and librarians, for a variety of teaching tools, visit us at
www.randomhouse.com/teachers

Published simultaneously in the United States and Canada

BANTAM SKYLARK is an imprint of Random House Children's Books, a divi-
sion of Random House, Inc. SKYLARK BOOK and colophon and BANTAM
BOOKS and colophon are registered trademarks of Random House, Inc.
Bantam Books, 1540 Broadway, New York, New York 10036.

PRINTED IN THE UNITED STATES OF AMERICA

CWO 10 9 8 7 6 5 4 3 2

For Bennett,

who will always be my baby

Hide and Peep

Chapter 1

Trina Larkspur yawned, a loud, open-mouthed yawn. It made everyone in the class turn to look at her.

"Oops!" The tiny fairy, three inchworms high, clapped a wing over her mouth. Serious Trina always tried to do her best at school.

"I'm sorry, Ms. Periwinkle," she told her first-grade teacher. "I'm just a little tired."

1

"That's all right, Trina." Ms. Periwinkle smiled. "I'm sure everyone in class is feeling sleepy. After all, it's not every day we start Fairy School at five-thirty in the morning!"

The first-grade class was gathered in the dark school meadow. They held paint-brushes and were ready to help grown-up fairies paint the sunrise. Bright fireflies had guided the students to school, and now they fluttered nearby, dimly lighting the circle of fairies. Trina dipped her brush into a can of bright red paint and waited.

"This is so exciting!" whispered her friend Olivia Skye. "Our first sunrise!" Olivia looked so wide-awake and happy, Trina grinned.

"Of course *you're* excited," Dorrie Windmist sighed. "Waking up in the middle of the night doesn't bother you at all—as long as you can be creative."

Dorrie tossed her long, messy curls and bumped against the yellow paint. "I was so tired this morning, I put on my sister's clothes instead of my own." She gazed at the too-big T-shirt and saw the paint spattered on it. "Uh-oh!" she yelped. "Arianna is going to be mad."

"What?" Belinda Dentalette bolted straight into the air. "Where am I?"

Usually Belinda was so full of energy she couldn't stop flapping her wings, but this morning she had fallen asleep against a daisy stem.

"It's okay," Trina assured her quickly. "We're just talking." She waved a wing at her three best friends, then at the school-tree behind them. "We're in Fairy School, Belinda. Remember?"

"Oh, that's right."

Just then a grown-up fairy painted the

4

first glow of dawn on the horizon, a small bright spot in the black sky. Ms. Periwinkle raised her hand and nodded to her students.

"This is it!" Trina told her friends. "Let's go!" All the fairies flew past the treetops to begin painting.

"Remember, broad clean strokes!" Ms. Perwinkle directed the class. "And work quickly. We don't have all day!"

Before Trina knew it, the sun was settled in the sky and the job was done. The fairy students thanked the grown-up sunrise fairies. Then they flew to their class branch in the Fairy School tree and slipped into seats behind toadstool-desks.

Dorrie turned to Trina. "What do you think we'll do for the rest of the morning?" she asked.

Olivia and Belinda leaned closer to listen. Trina was almost always right.

"Well, I've been doing a lot of reading about early-morning magic," Trina said. She'd read every book in the school library and was always looking for more things to learn. "We'll probably learn how to open flower petals that close at night."

"How do you do that?" Belinda asked.

"You sing a good-morning song. Softly at first. Then you sing a little louder until the flower wakes up. I've already made up a song, just in case we have the lesson. My song is about waving good-bye to the moon."

"No wonder you're the best student in school!" Dorrie said admiringly.

A few seats away, another fairy snorted.

"Do you have a problem, Laurel?" Belinda demanded.

"Humph!" Mean little Laurel turned

up her nose. She couldn't stand it when another fairy got a compliment. "Everyone may *think* Trina is the best student," she said. "But I think she's just lucky!"

"All right, everyone!" Ms. Periwinkle called from the front of the branch. "We're ready to begin our next lesson."

Trina turned her back to Laurel. She wasn't about to let the other fairy bother her. "La, de dum," she hummed to herself, rehearsing the good-morning song she'd composed. She was sure that was what they'd do next. She took out a lilypad-notebook, already marked EARLY MORNING.

"We're about to start a brand-new project," Ms. Periwinkle announced after they'd recited the Fairy School Pledge. "It's a different direction for our class, one that will surprise everyone."

She smiled at Trina. "You can put that notebook away, Trina. You won't be needing it."

Trina's eyes opened wide in amazement.

"See that, Ms. Smarty-Wings?" Laurel sneered. "Even a brilliant fairy like you can be wrong!"

Chapter 2

Laurel had spoken so loudly, Trina was sure everyone in class had heard the insult. But she refused to let her wings droop from embarrassment.

Let Laurel make fun of me, she thought. No matter what the project is, I'm going to work at it and work at it and work at it!

She tilted her head toward Ms. Periwinkle so she wouldn't miss a word.

"We'll be learning more about nature," the teacher was explaining, "by helping young animals to grow. We'll raise them here in Fairyland and then take them to Earth-Below."

She rubbed her wings together. "You'll each get a journal to fill in. You'll be graded on the information you record about your animal's growth and development and how well your animal adjusts to life in Fairyland. Let's get started!"

Dorrie craned her neck and looked all around. "But I don't see any animals!"

"Patience, please," Ms. Periwinkle said. She tossed some fairy dust into the air and giant magic globes appeared, bobbing outside the class branch. Each globe had a pair of animals inside: two wriggling puppies taking first steps. Two eggs about to hatch into chicks. Two baby robins in a nest, their eyes shut tight. Two pink-skinned baby mice. Two kittens like little balls of fur. Two baby snakes, twined around each other.

"You'll notice there are two of each animal," Ms. Periwinkle added. "So you can compare them as they grow. Now, let's all fly to the school meadow. In just a few minutes, the globes will melt away and your babies will float next to you on the soft grass."

Trina gazed at the globes as she fluttered to the ground. It seemed strange to think that she was supposed to take care of one of these animals. They were all bigger than the tallest little fairy!

When all the fairies had landed, Ms. Periwinkle waved her magic wand. *"Magic globes now disappear. Baby animals stay right here,"* she recited.

A soft glow fell over the globes and they vanished. One egg hovered over Trina. She watched it sway back and forth, then slowly drift down and settle next to her on the grass.

"Oh!" she breathed softly. She put her arms around the giant egg.

All at once the egg trembled. Trina jumped. The egg teetered dangerously, then righted itself.

"Ms. Periwinkle?" she called in a shaky voice.

"It's all right," Ms. Periwinkle said, hurrying over. "The egg is just fine."

"You mean little Ms. Smarty-Wings got an egg too?" Laurel chuckled. "But *she* almost smashed hers. I'd never do that!"

Trina whirled around. The other egg stood next to Laurel.

"Nothing really happened," Trina said, defending herself.

"Sure, sure," Laurel said. "Keep telling

yourself that." Then she tickled her egg. "Come out, baby chick," she cooed. "Laurel's waiting for you!"

Crack! The egg split neatly in two and a fuzzy yellow chick popped out. "Peep!" the chick said.

"Hello, chickie!" Laurel peeped back, loudly enough for Trina to hear. "Welcome to Fairyland! I think I'll call you Clarice."

All around Trina, fairies were getting to know their babies, talking and playing and having fun.

Belinda was placing a baby robin in a cozy nest. "I can't wait to teach you to fly," she told the bird softly.

Dorrie stroked a bright orange kitten. "Oh, Kitty," she sighed happily. "You're the sweetest animal in the world!"

"Look at these brilliant colors!" Olivia exclaimed as she made her baby snake comfortable in the grass. "This snake has the prettiest design I've ever seen."

Everyone was working with their babies. Everyone but Trina.

"Excuse me, Ms. Periwinkle?" she called. "Why hasn't my egg hatched?"

The teacher flipped through some pages in a notebook. "Hmmm. Your baby chick should have hatched today. But maybe it needs a little more time."

"More time?" It didn't seem fair. Other fairies were busy scribbling in their journals, already working on the assignment. And Trina hadn't done one thing—except almost break her egg. She was behind before she'd even begun.

Ms. Periwinkle nodded. "Why don't you figure out how to keep the egg warm for tonight? Then we'll see what happens in the morning."

Good, Trina thought. Something to do. She darted quickly to the class branch. She grabbed her magic wand and some fairy dust. Then she flew back to the egg and thought for a moment.

"Egg needs a blanket for the cool, cool night. Make it warm and make it bright," she chanted, waving her wand.

A soft green blanket made from moss floated over and draped itself around the egg.

"There," Trina said, satisfied. "Now I'll just measure the egg and record the size in my journal."

Trina tossed some fairy dust. The dust formed a long measuring tape and wound itself around the egg. Trina made some notes in her journal.

Laurel peeked over Trina's shoulder and yawned. "Boring!" Her baby chick waddled close behind. "But I don't really blame you, Trina. What else could you do with just an egg?"

Trina thought for a second, then smiled. There really was nothing else to do for her egg, which meant she'd have an extra day to do some research. She'd learn everything she could about how chicks grow. As soon as the school bell chimed, she'd rush right off to the library.

"Don't worry about me," Trina told Laurel. "My chick will be the most amazing animal of all."

Chapter 3

B-r-r-i-i-ng! The school bell chimed.

"Let's go!" Trina said to her friends. "Who's coming with me to the library to do some animal research?"

Dorrie shook her head. "Ms. Periwinkle said we can stay late and play with our animals. I think I'll do that."

The first-grade fairies had set up a nursery in the school meadow, filled with birds'

18

nests, snake pits, mouse holes, and kitten and puppy baskets.

"Me too," said Belinda, hopping up and down. "My baby bird doesn't like to be alone, so I'm going to stay with her as long as I can. At least until dinner."

Trina turned hopefully to Olivia. "Sorry, Belinda," Olivia said softly. "I'm going home to fairy-sit for Nicholas and Natalia. We're going to come right back here so they can see the baby animals."

Trina shrugged. "Well, I'll go by myself then." She eyed her egg, just sitting there, doing nothing. "Hurry up and hatch," she whispered. "And then we can really get to work!"

✳✳✳

A little while later, Trina sat in the living room of her tree-house with a towering

19

stack of books in front of her. She had checked out every book on chicks she could find in the library. *Raising Baby Chicks, How Chicks Grow, From Chick to Chicken.* There were so many books, she had to make three trips to fly them all home.

"Let's see," she said out loud. "Where should I begin?"

She had tons to learn! She opened the first book and began to read: "Baby chickens take three weeks to hatch from eggs . . ."

"Trina Larkspur!" her mom exclaimed a few hours later. "Why are you reading in the dark?"

Trina blinked. It *was* dark. It must be dinnertime by now. She flipped on a firefly lamp beside her. "I didn't realize how late it was," she said.

She quickly told her mother about the new school project. "Laurel's chick is so cute and cuddly," she said. "She already follows Laurel everywhere. But with all this research I'm doing, I bet my chick will grow to be a superchicken!"

Mrs. Larkspur smiled. "Well, right now I'm a little worried about *my* superfairy. You've been reading for hours. You know, Trina, some things you just can't learn from a book. And you won't be able to teach it all to your chick in a few days. Why don't you be patient and see what your chick can teach you?"

Trina nodded. But she didn't really believe her mom. So after dinner she stayed up late, poring over chapter after chapter in her books.

She finally went to sleep. At dawn's early light her eyes flew open. Her egg had probably hatched by now! She scribbled a note for her sleeping parents, then rushed off to school.

A few minutes later she skidded to a stop in the school meadow. There was her egg— still whole and unbroken.

Trina sighed and sat down next to it. She'd wait here and not move until it cracked.

One by one the other fairies arrived at the meadow. They waited for their animals to wake up. Then they fed them, talked to them, and played with them.

"Watch out for your puppy!" Dorrie shouted to a fairy named Sebastian. "He almost squished me with his paw!"

"Sorry," said Sebastian. "He's just learning how to walk. He's not that steady yet."

"You must be careful," Ms. Periwinkle warned, flying close to the fairies. "These animals are much larger than we are. You must teach them to be respectful of all living things, no matter how small."

"Well, my chick is perfectly trained already," Laurel boasted. "She follows me everywhere and does whatever I say."

Trina sighed. "Laurel's chick is so advanced," she said to Dorrie. "And my chick hasn't even hatched!"

"But everything you do turns out perfectly," Dorrie told her. "You just wait and see." Then she faced her kitten and showed her how to clean herself. Suddenly her kitten bolted to chase a butterfly. "Wait, Kitty!" Dorrie shouted. "Wait for me!"

Trina turned to Belinda, who was standing in front of her robin and flapping her wings. "This is how you fly, Robby," Belinda said. But then Kitty rolled into Robby and the two began to play.

Belinda and Dorrie raced after their animals, forgetting about Trina and her egg.

Now there was nothing to do and no one

to talk to. Trina placed her books around the egg. When the chick hatched, it could look at the pictures and learn what it was supposed to do. Then Trina watched Laurel.

"All right, Clarice," Laurel was saying. "Fetch my magic wand from my fairypack."

Clarice bobbed her head, then hurried to the fairypack. She rooted around with her beak. Finally she found the wand and held it gently until she dropped it—right on Laurel's head.

Trina giggled. Well, at least Clarice wasn't absolutely perfect.

"Just one more lesson, and Clarice will be an expert at doing exactly what I tell her," Laurel said in a huff. "Isn't this animal project great?"

Then Laurel eyed Trina's unbroken egg. "Well, maybe not for everyone," she added.

Crack! Trina jumped up. Could it be? Was

it time for her chick to hatch? *Crack! Crack!* Trina peered closely at her egg. Yes, there was a hole in the middle of the shell, and a chick—her chick!—was peeking out.

"Hi," Trina said softly. Finally her chick was coming. What would she be like? Or maybe it would be a he. It would be soft and cuddly, she felt sure, and eager to learn everything Trina could teach it.

The chick pecked at the shell. Trina grabbed her magic wand and rapped it hard against the shell to speed things up.

"Ouch!" cried the chick in a surprisingly deep voice. "Watch the stick, fairy!"

Chapter 4

What a strange-sounding chick! But at least one of Trina's questions was answered. Her chick was a boy.

The chick tossed his head, and the top of the shell flew off. Then he tumbled out, fluttering his wet, sticky wings and spraying Trina and a few nearby fairies with yellow yolk.

"Yuck!" she couldn't help exclaiming.

"Hey, chick! Watch it!" Laurel snapped.

Trina's chick chuckled. "You look good in yellow," he told Laurel. "It must be your color. And that's no yolk!"

What? Her chick was joking with Laurel? The meanest, most wisecracking fairy in Fairy School?

Laurel scowled at the chick for a second before she turned back to Clarice with a "Humph."

Belinda, Olivia, and Dorrie hurried to Trina's side with napkin-leaves, wiping her off as best they could.

"Thanks," Trina told them. She eyed her chick as it rolled around in the broken bits of shell, not the least bit interested in Trina or the research books she'd spread out. "This isn't going to be easy."

She gazed at the kitten and the robin, playing quietly near Dorrie and Belinda.

Even Olivia's snake, its colors shining brilliantly in the sun, seemed like a better project than her chick.

"You'll figure something out," Belinda told her. "You always do."

Trina brightened. "I'll just check what the books say." She hurried to her pile of notes and books and began to flip through pages.

"Hey, fairy!" the chick called out to her. "Can I get some help standing up?"

Trina dropped the books. "Of course!" She flapped around the chick, tugging here, pushing there, and finally the chick stood wobbling on two feet.

"I'll be right back." Trina hurried back to her books and quickly read a passage. "I need to spread leaves and paper for you to lie down on when you're tired," she explained to the chick.

"Leaves and paper?" the chick repeated.

"What about that soft moss blanket that covered my egg? That would be nice to rest on."

Trina shook her head. "No, that's too slippery for you. All the books say you need to stay on leaves and keep warm."

She took out her magic wand. *"Trees, send your leaves from up in the air. Send them down for my chick to share."*

Handfuls of leaves fluttered to the ground, falling around the baby animal.

"Achoo!" The chick sneezed as a leaf tickled his nose.

"There," Trina said, satisfied. "Now I need to make sure the air temperature is exactly eighty-five degrees. Otherwise, you might catch a chill."

She tossed a handful of fairy dust. The dust sprinkled over the chick, then disappeared. Waves of heat circled the baby animal, and he blinked in surprise.

"Whew!" The chick wiped a wing across his face. "I feel like I'm sitting in a furnace! Can't you cool it just a little?"

"Sorry," Trina told him. "All the books say you need to stay in eighty-five-degree temperature until you grow a bit bigger." The chick didn't look happy about it. Maybe she could distract him with a special treat. "How about something to eat?"

The chick perked up. "Great! What's on the menu?"

"Sunflower seeds," said Trina. "Excuse me!" she called to a sunflower that was bending in the breeze a few feet away. "Could you please send some seeds our way?"

The chick turned up his nose. "Don't bother," he shouted to the flower. "I'm not

31

really interested in seeds." He turned to Kitty, who was lapping at a seashell filled with milk. "I'd like some of that instead."

"Milk?" Trina exclaimed. "Chicks don't drink milk. You're supposed to eat sunflower seeds!"

"No way, fairy. No seeds for me."

Trina sighed. Her animal project was only a few minutes old, and she was already frustrated. Why wouldn't this chick do things by the book?

Chapter 5

Every day that week, the first-grade fairies cared for the young animals. The feathers on Trina's chick fluffed out, and he began to walk steadily on his own. But he didn't seem interested in pecking at things, or scratching around in the dirt, or anything that Laurel's chick was doing. Instead, he'd roll around with the kittens or puppies or flap his wings with the baby birds.

What was going on?

One morning, Trina noted his new height in her lilypad, then buried her nose in the stack of books beside her.

The other fairies were playing with their animals, having fun while Trina studied.

"Hey, Trina," Dorrie said, flying over. "What are you doing?"

"Research," Trina explained, barely looking up. "I ordered all these books from a messenger fairy. Maybe they'll help me figure out how to get this chick to do what he's supposed to."

"What do you mean?"

"Well, chicks are supposed to drink water. But all he wants is your kitten's milk. And he should be eating small stones. But he only wants that baby mouse's cheese!"

She pointed her wing at her chick, who was now hopping after another fairy and his mouse. "And no matter how many times I tell him he can't fly yet, he still flaps his wings like Robby."

Dorrie thought a moment. Her kitten settled cozily beside her, and she sighed happily. "Hi, Kitty," she said softly. "Hey!" she said suddenly to Trina. "Maybe if you name your chick, he'll feel better. Maybe then he'll do what you want."

Trina opened a new book and quickly read through the chapter titles. "No. None of these books say anything about names." She closed the book, then caught sight of the thermometer she kept dangling near the chick at all times.

"Oh, no!" she said. "It's only eighty degrees! He must be freezing. All the books say a mother hen sits on her chicks when they're cold."

Trina darted over to her chick. She

plopped onto his back. He flapped his wings, and she slid right off.

"No chicken rides, fairy," the chick told her, "until I get my milk and cheese!"

***

A few minutes later, Ms. Periwinkle called the class to the first-grade branch. The fairies had wish-granting and cloud-shaping lessons. But Trina couldn't stop thinking about her chick. She'd just have to try harder to make him a proper chick. Otherwise, she'd have nothing good to write in her journal. She'd think and think and work and work and study even harder and come up with answers.

At recess, everyone flew to the meadow to give their animals lunch and make sure they were exercising.

"I'm going to have my chick march in a

straight line," Trina told Dorrie. "It'll be good discipline and good exercise."

"Your chick can exercise just by running around with his friends," Dorrie said. "Don't you want him to have fun?"

"Fun?" Trina tugged on her ear. "I want my chick to be healthy!"

"Of course you do," Dorrie said quickly. Then she called out, "Kitty! Time to roll around with some fairy yarn!"

"Goody!" the kitten said, padding over.

Trina watched them play for a moment. It did look like fun. But exercise was serious business. "Here, chick!" she shouted. "Get ready to march."

When the chick hopped over, she clapped her hands in a steady rhythm. "I want you to march in time to my claps," she said. "Legs high. Head up. Shoulders back."

"I don't think I have shoulders," said the chick. "Besides, I want to play!"

Trina frowned. This project was going terribly. Her journal was practically empty. She felt too silly to put in how the chick played like a kitten. So she'd only recorded height and weight. What kind of grade would she get for that?

She gazed around, desperate for her chick to do something—anything a chick would do.

Then her eyes fell on Laurel and Clarice. "I know!" she said. "Let's play with them so you can learn proper chick behavior!"

"Okay!" The chick brightened, happy he'd be playing.

Trina joined a surprised Laurel and Clarice. "We're playing hide-and-seek!" Clarice chirped gaily.

"Can we play too?" asked Trina's chick.

"Sure!" Clarice agreed before Laurel could say no.

"Well?" Trina said to Laurel.

Laurel shrugged. "I guess your chick can look for you while Clarice looks for me. Then you can see how much better I'm doing on this project. Okay," she instructed. "You chicks cover your eyes and Trina and I will hide."

Feeling silly, Trina found the chicks' old eggshells behind some tall blades of grass. "This is a good place to hide," she told herself, and crouched inside one.

Trina sat for a long while. The chicks passed by once, and she kept quiet. But they never came back. She waited and waited and waited, but the chicks still didn't come. It seemed like ages had passed since they'd started the game.

Finally she heard flaps and a giggle. At last! thought Trina. My chick will find me, and then we can start marching.

But it was only Laurel, peeking into the shell. The mean fairy pointed at Trina and shook with laughter. "Clarice, perfect little Clarice, found me an hour ago. But your chick never started looking for you," Laurel sneered. "He's chasing Frisbees with the puppy and forgot all about you."

Chapter 6

Trina's chick didn't like her. That was clear. And he still hadn't done anything like the books said he should, so Trina had nothing to record. Her journal was still practically empty.

What was wrong with her chick? For the first time ever, Trina felt like a failure in school.

"What am I going to do?" she asked her

friends as they flew off the class branch at the end of the day. "We don't have much time left with our animals before we take them to Earth-Below."

It was so odd for Trina to be asking for advice! Belinda, Olivia, and Dorrie just shook their heads.

"I don't know, Trina," Belinda finally said. "Maybe you should talk to Ms. Periwinkle. She helped me when I had trouble with tooth fairy class."

Trina stopped in midair. "That's a great idea, Belinda! I'll go talk to her right now."

"You mean you're not coming to play by the weeping willow tree?" said Dorrie. The four fairies played under the tree's canopy of leaves practically every day. "You've been doing so much work for this project, Mr. Willow hasn't seen you all week."

"Yesterday he couldn't stop crying, he

missed you so much." Olivia paused a moment, then added, "I know he's always sobbing, but yesterday it was so bad, we had to open umbrellas!"

"Tell him I'll see him when this school project is over," Trina said. "But right now I have to see Ms. Periwinkle!"

Trina flew as fast as she could back to Fairy School. Luckily the teacher was still at her desk, going over the journals from the fairies.

"Hello, Trina," Ms. Periwinkle said. "How's your journal?"

"That's why I'm here, Ms. Periwinkle!" Trina said quickly. "I did lots of research, but I've been having problems with this project. My chick doesn't listen to me. He won't do anything right. How can I write that he likes milk and cheese and playing with yarn?"

Ms. Periwinkle shook her head. "Sometimes things don't go exactly as you plan, no matter how hard you try. Just because your chick is different, that doesn't mean he's wrong. It sounds like he's a special chick and he needs some special attention."

Trina squinched her forehead and thought hard for a second. "I think I understand, Ms. Periwinkle. I've been forcing my chick to be something he doesn't want to be, and that's making us both unhappy. I should be writing down whatever he does even if it's un-chicklike?"

"Exactly!" Ms. Periwinkle agreed. "I bet you'll have a more interesting journal than you do right now."

"Too bad I figured this out on the next-to-last day."

Ms. Periwinkle fluttered her wings. "But, Trina, we don't leave for Earth-Below until

46

school ends the day after tomorrow. You can spend the next two days with your chick. Remember, this assignment isn't about raising the perfect animal, but studying what makes each animal special."

Trina flapped her wings with excitement. "Thank you, Ms. Periwinkle! I'll see you tomorrow."

She soared off the branch and hovered for a moment above the school meadow. She could see her chick squeezed in between the two kittens, lapping at a big nutshell filled with milk.

She remembered what Ms. Periwinkle had said: "The assignment is to study what makes each animal special." And her chick was special, all right. Not like any other chick under the sun.

"Of course!" Trina shouted. "He's playing

with the kittens. Lately that's all he's been doing. Playing and acting like a kitten. I should have been reading up on them!

She rushed to the library. She'd have to read fast if she wanted to make her last two days with her chick the best they could be!

Chapter 7

Trina brought home armloads of kitten books from the library. She settled on her leaf-bed and opened the first one. Quickly she scanned the pages: How they walk. How they play. Every time she saw a trait her chick had too, she laughed out loud.

"Kittens press against someone and purr as a sign of affection," she read.

Trina giggled, remembering the chick

rubbing against her leg every morning when she gave him breakfast. He was only saying thank you! And she never said you're welcome! She was going to rush over to the basket where he was staying with the other kittens right now and apologize! If he wanted to be a kitten, that was perfectly fine with her.

Trina darted out her knothole window and raced to the school meadow. "Hi!" she said, settling on the ground next to the chick. She peered into the basket. "Would you like me to scratch your ears? Get some yarn for you to play with? Drink some milk?"

The chick lifted his head. "Do you know what I'd really like to do?"

"Clean your paws? Chase some mice?"

"Be a bird."

"A bird?" Trina was confused for a sec-

and I've already gotten A's in all my other assignments."

At last, too tired to work a minute more, Trina closed her eyes.

Boom! A bolt of lightning split the sky. Trina jumped awake. Rain poured down in buckets. Trina shivered as a gust of cold air blasted into the room.

It was a thunderstorm.

"Oh, no!" she cried. "My chick! My poor little chick! He's stuck in a birds' nest, and he can't fly to shelter!"

Not wasting a second, Trina rushed outside. She didn't think about her own warmth or safety. She was too worried about her chick. How could she have thought he was just an assignment?

She beat her wings frantically against the powerful wind. She had to get to her chick in time. She had to!

Chapter 8

Trina hurled herself against the rain and wind. Raindrops as large as seashells smashed against her wings. Gusts twirled her around and around, and she could hardly see through the stormy night.

"Oh, please, please let my chick be okay," she said to herself. "Let me get there in time."

She peered through the mist. And there,

up ahead, was Fairy School. She knew her chick's nest was right next door.

Trina flapped her wings, faster and faster. She spied the tiny nest high up in a tree. The mighty wind bent the branch almost in two. The nest shook but still clung to the branch by a few twigs.

She could see her chick's yellow head poking out from the leaves. He was shaking with fear!

"I'm coming!" she called to her chick. But her shouts were lost in the wind and noise.

She took one big breath, then swooped close to the nest.

All at once, lightning struck the tree. The branch snapped in half.

"Heeeelp!" cried the chick, toppling out of the nest. He dropped like a stone.

In a flash, Trina dove under the chick and caught him just before he hit the ground.

Rain poured down all around them, but it was okay. Her chick was okay!

"Oh, Buster!" Trina cradled the chick in her arms. "Are you all right?"

The chick sighed. He nestled cozily under Trina's wing. "My name is Buster?" he said faintly.

"I guess so," Trina laughed, and hugged him tight. "And now, Buster, you're coming home with me."

***

Back at her tree-house, Trina spread a blanket of moss on the living room floor. Outside, thunder rumbled and lightning lit the sky. But inside, Trina and Buster snuggled together and all was peaceful.

"Oh, Buster," Trina said. "I was so worried about you."

"You were?" Buster said, surprised. "I

thought you didn't care about me because I did everything wrong!"

"Of course I care! I just didn't know how much until you were in danger. And you weren't doing anything wrong. I didn't realize it was okay for you to be different. You were only trying to find out what you should do and how you should act so you would be happy. Sure, you aren't an ordinary chick. But you were just trying to learn! And I didn't realize you could learn things that way—and not just from books!"

"I'm just different . . . and that's okay . . . I can be anything I want to be . . ." Buster mumbled as he yawned, then drifted off to sleep.

Trina looked at Buster, who was snoring just a bit, and smiled. She patted his soft feathers and thought how she'd miss him when he went to Earth-Below.

How could I think he was only a school project? she wondered. Or that he needed to be just like any other chick, straight out of a book? He wasn't just a bunch of animal traits. He was a living, breathing creature. And he needed love and care.

He was Buster. Her Buster. The funniest, silliest, most amazing chick around.

Chapter 9

At breakfast, Mr. and Mrs. Larkspur were surprised to see Buster. But they made room for their guest, pushing aside extra chairs so the chick could squeeze in at their walnut table.

"What would you like for breakfast, Buster?" Mr. Larkspur asked. "I think we have some extra milk and cream."

"No, thanks," Trina answered quickly. "But do you have any bird feed?"

"Excuse me," Buster said, eyeing a shell-plate stacked with Pixie Pancakes. "I'd like to try some of those."

Trina laughed. Something different again!

After breakfast, they walked to Fairy School together. "Oh, poor Trina," Laurel said with a sneer as they neared the school-tree. "Having to take care of her chick who thinks he's not a chick. Your school project was one big joke! Not like my sweet Clarice!"

Trina just laughed. Let Laurel make fun and think she had the perfect chick. Buster was terrific, no matter what anyone thought.

Hours passed, and just as Ms. Periwinkle had promised, the fairies spent the entire day with their baby animals. Trina observed Buster at work and play. He helped Robby take apart the birds' nests. Then he and Kitty wound up the balls of yarn, putting them away. He even waddled over to Clarice and brushed up the leaves and papers she used for her coop.

Why, he has grown up, Trina realized. And he's a good friend to all the other animals.

She reached for her journal, then stopped herself. She didn't have much time left with Buster. Why use it writing in her journal, when she could fill it in later?

Cuckoo! A cuckoo-clock bird flew past and everyone counted off the time. "All right, class," Ms. Periwinkle called. "Three o'clock! It's time to finish up here and head down to Earth-Below."

The teacher waved her magic wand. The magic globes appeared again, this time circling each pair: fairy and baby animal.

"These globes will float you to the right

place," Ms. Periwinkle told the class, "then fade away. After you've settled your animals where they belong, everyone please meet at the foot of the Rainbow Bridge, and we'll travel home together."

Standing wing to wing, Trina and her chick floated past clouds and birds and butterflies, slowly floating down the Rainbow Bridge to a farm on Earth-Below.

Seconds later, Trina spied a chicken yard with lots of fluffy chicks running around. *Pop!* The globe disappeared, and Trina and Buster stood on the ground.

"Well, we're here," Trina said. "It's time to say good-bye."

She felt a lump in her throat, and a tear trickled down her cheek.

"Now, don't get all sappy on me," Buster told her. He tried to smile but wound up sniffling instead.

One of the hens was waving at Buster and jumping up and down. Trina knew she had to leave.

"You go on," she told Buster, nudging him forward. "Go make some friends!"

The chick waved a stubby wing as he moved slowly forward. "Thanks for being my first friend," he called back to Trina.

Buster turned and joined the chicks. "I'm Buster," she heard him say.

Trina smiled. He would have a good home now. And lots of new friends. Trina wished she could stay longer. But she had to hurry back to the Rainbow Bridge to join her class.

She had plenty of work ahead of her too. Plenty of entries for her journal. Of course she'd tell about Buster sleeping in a nest and purring like a cat. That was all part of Buster and part of how he grew.

And even if it wasn't what everyone was expecting . . . even if it wasn't by the book . . . who cared?

Trina had done more than a school project. She'd helped raise a baby chick!

The Fairy School Pledge

(sung to the tune of "Twinkle, Twinkle, Little Star")

We are fairies
Brave and bright.
Shine by day,
Twinkle by night.

We're friends of birds
And kind to bees.
We love flowers
And the trees.

We are fairies
Brave and bright.
Shine by day,
Twinkle by night.